To Teacher Joan, who loves pets
D. D.

In memory of my beloved friend Trina
M. H.

Text copyright © 2006 by Dayle Ann Dodds
Illustrations copyright © 2006 by Marylin Hafner

First edition 2006

Library of Congress Cataloging-in-Publication Data is available

Library of Congress Catalog Card Number 2005053186

ISBN 0-7636-2252-4

2 4 6 8 10 9 7 5 3 1

Printed in China

This book was typeset in Clichee.
The illustrations were done in ink, watercolor, and colored pencil.

Candlewick Press
2067 Massachusetts Avenue
Cambridge, Massachusetts 02140

visit us at www.candlewick.com

Teacher's Pets

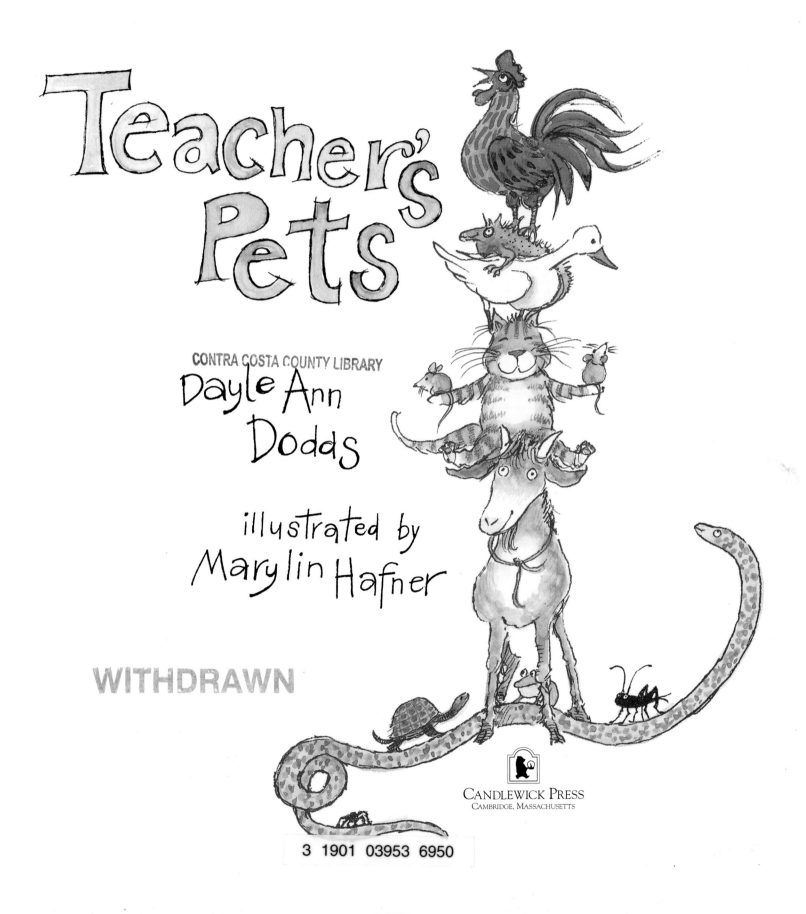

Dayle Ann Dodds

illustrated by Marylin Hafner

CANDLEWICK PRESS
CAMBRIDGE, MASSACHUSETTS

Monday was sharing day in Miss Fry's class.
"You may bring something special," said Miss Fry.

"May we share a pet?" Winston asked.

"Yes," said Miss Fry. "But just for the day."

COOL!

On Monday, Winston brought in his pet rooster.
"I call him Red. He eats corn, and he crows.
The neighbors say he crows too much."

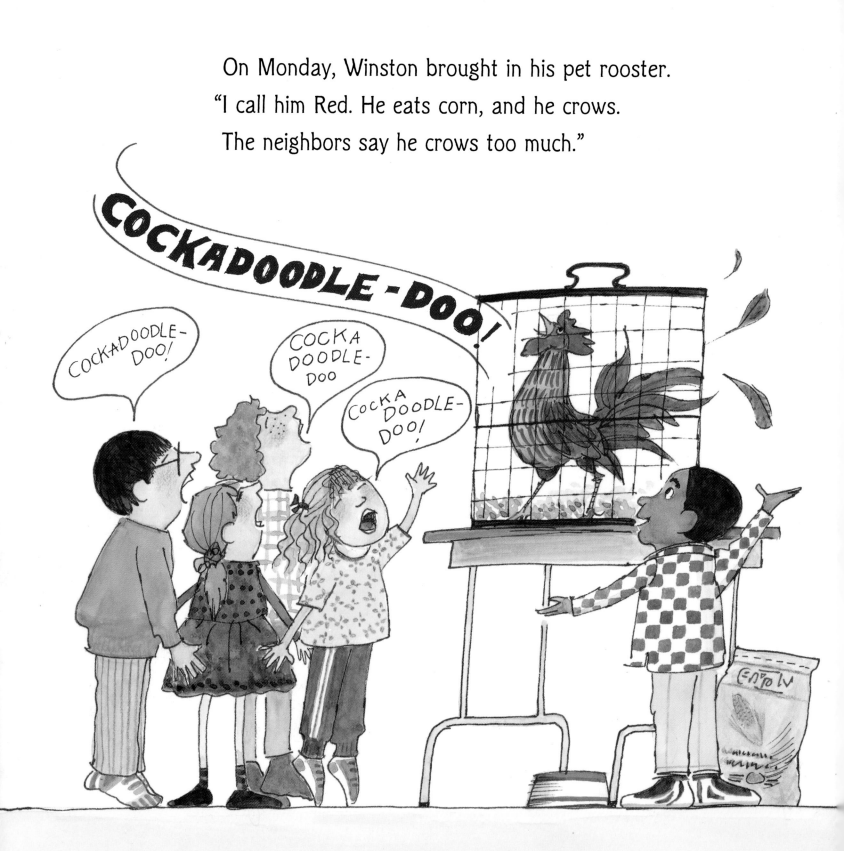

"What a wonderful pet," said Miss Fry.
"We're happy he can visit us today."

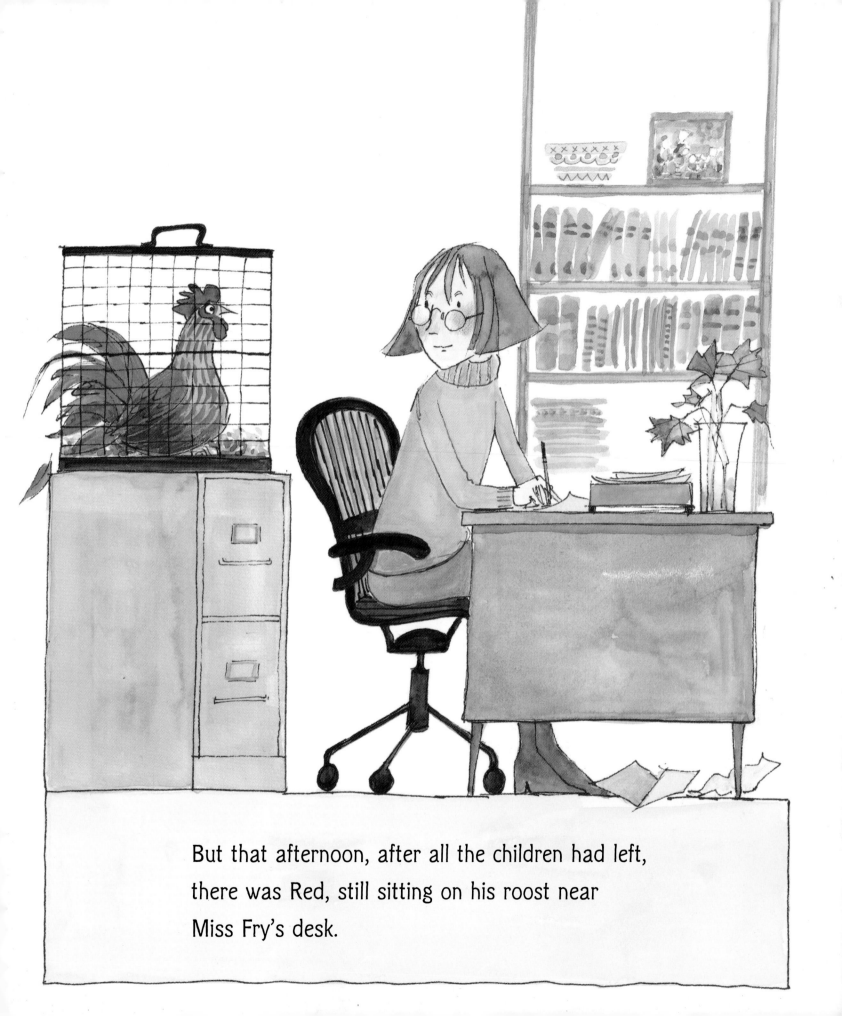

But that afternoon, after all the children had left,
there was Red, still sitting on his roost near
Miss Fry's desk.

She sprinkled corn in Red's dish,
then locked the door and went home
to her quiet little house.

On Tuesday, Winston told Miss Fry, "The neighbors wonder if Red can stay at school for a while."

"Of course," said Miss Fry. "How lucky for us."

$$6 \times 1 = 6$$
$$6 \times 2 = 12$$

The next Monday was Patrick's turn. "My tarantula's name is Vincent. He likes to eat bugs and hide inside my mother's slippers."

"What a wonderful pet," said Miss Fry. "Don't forget to take Vincent home with you at the end of the day."

But that afternoon, after all the children had left, there was Vincent, still sitting in his jar on Miss Fry's desk.

She gave Vincent a big juicy bug, sprinkled corn in Red's dish, then locked the door and went home to her quiet little house.

On Tuesday, Patrick told Miss Fry, "My mother says Vincent likes her slippers too much. We're wondering if he can stay at school for a few days."

"Of course," said Miss Fry. "How lucky for us."

The next week, Roger brought in his cricket.
"His name is Moe," said Roger. "He eats leaves from
the garden and sings *chirrup-chirrup* all night long."

"What a wonderful pet," said Miss Fry.

That afternoon, after all the children had left,
Miss Fry noticed Moe sitting in his box on the table.

Miss Fry looked at Moe. He almost seemed to smile.
"Welcome to our class, Moe."

Right before her eyes,
he did a huge somersault—
up, up in the air.

"Bravo!" said Miss Fry.

She gave fresh green leaves to Moe
and a big juicy bug to Vincent, sprinkled
corn in Red's dish, then locked the door
and went home to her quiet little house.

The next day, Roger said to Miss Fry, "My mother says
Moe chirps too much."

"He's welcome to visit as long as he likes," said Miss Fry.

And so it went.

Alia shared her pet goat named
Gladys. It said *Baaaaaa!* and ate
her sister's homework.

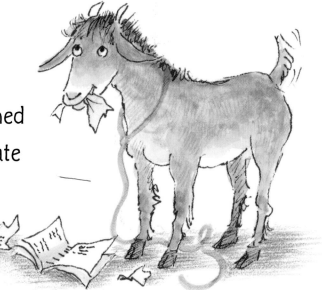

Amanda shared her pet dachshund.
It liked to chew bones and the pillows
on her aunt Judy's new sofa.

Jerry brought in his pet boa constrictor.
It never made a sound. No one knew
exactly what it liked to eat, but Jerry
said his father's expensive tropical fish
had suddenly disappeared one day.

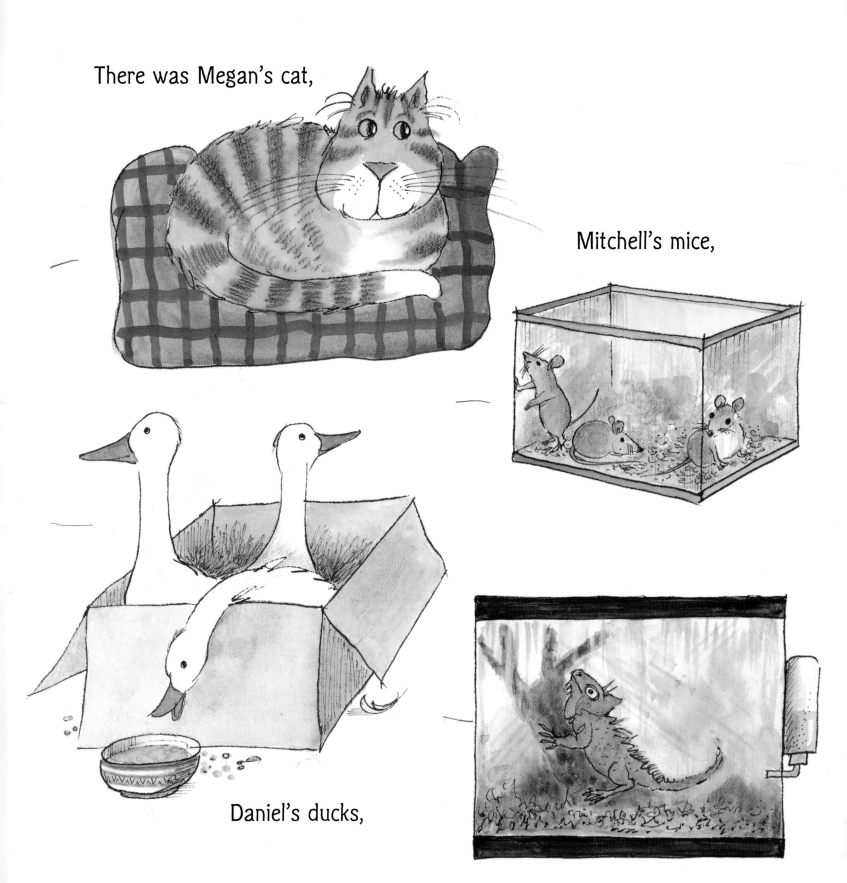

There was Megan's cat,

Mitchell's mice,

Daniel's ducks,

and Tom's iguana.

Lily's monkey,

Frankie's frog,

Terrence's turtle . . .

and something square and fuzzy that Avery
brought in.

"It looks like a kitchen sponge," said Bruce.
"A *really old* kitchen sponge."

"It's my pet," said Avery, and that was that.

Before long, Miss Fry's classroom was bursting with
the happy noises of all the children's pets.

On Parents' Night, the mothers and
fathers walked around the classroom
with great big smiles on their faces.

"Isn't it great," they said, "that Miss Fry
loves pets so?"

chirrup

Only Roger's cricket sat quietly in his box. "You must miss your garden," Miss Fry said.

Chirrup, Moe said softly. He crawled under one of his shiny green leaves.

On the last day of school,
Miss Fry's class had a party
with balloons, hats, and
ice-cream cups.

"Goodbye, children!" Miss Fry sang out.
"Have a nice summer . . . *and don't forget to*

take home your pets!

I sure won't.

One by one, the children disappeared, and with them went their pets.

"No more pets," said Miss Fry. She looked around the quiet, empty room.

Then Miss Fry noticed a box sitting on her desk.

She peeked inside. A little face
looked up at her. It almost seemed
to smile.

A note inside read:

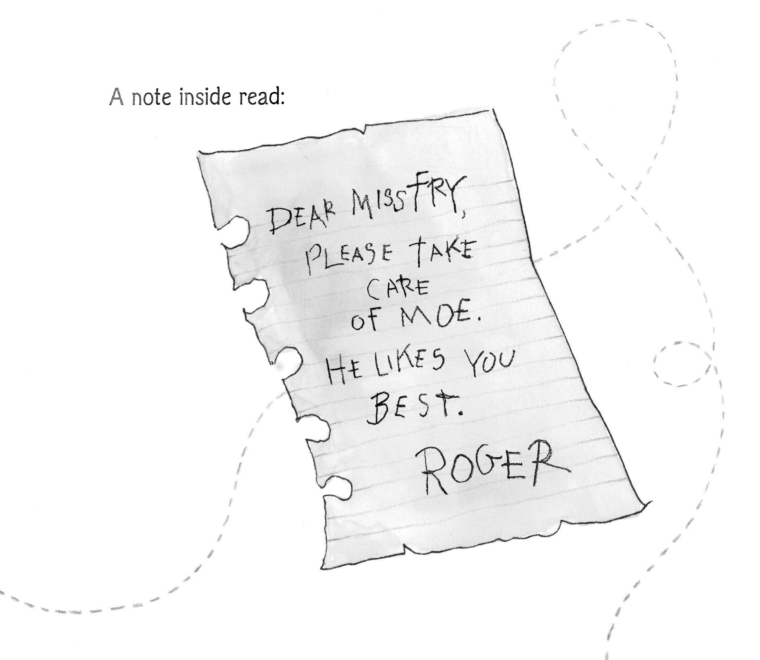

DEAR MISS FRY,
PLEASE TAKE
CARE
OF MOE.

HE LIKES YOU
BEST.

ROGER

"How lucky for me," said Miss Fry.

Moe did a huge somersault—up, up
in the air.

Miss Fry carried her new pet to her quiet little house and placed him in the garden, among the rainbow of roses.

That night, Miss Fry opened her window.

She climbed into bed.

She turned off the lamp.

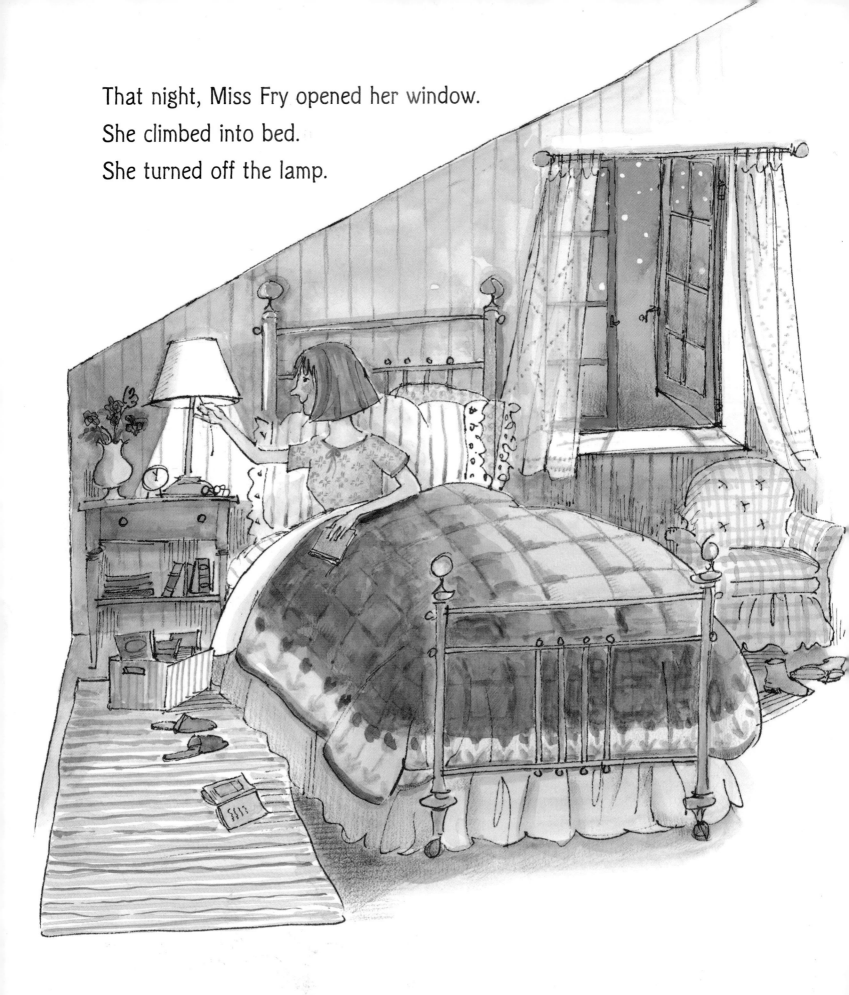

By the light of the moon,
from outside in the garden,
came a happy noise.

Chirrup-chirrup!

chirrup!